The Worry Warriors

Written by Tarnelia Matthews

Illustrated by Maïté Schmitt

Collins

1 The audition

Eden stood in front of the poster and gulped. The teachers were already calling out surnames beginning with C, which meant hers would be coming next; her palms were getting sweaty just thinking about it. Standing in front of her bedroom mirror belting out songs was one thing, but the thought of singing in front of Mr Pink and his piano, whilst the rest of the school year watched, made her feel very queasy.

"Martin Collins – "

Mr Pink's deep voice echoed across the hall and Martin, a spectacled boy, nervously made his way to the front. The only reason why Eden was able to make it out of the hall was by asking to use the toilet and she knew she couldn't hang about there forever; she needed a plan and fast!

That's when she remembered – the props room! A space so cluttered and stacked with boxes, that you could easily hide from anyone. That's where she would escape the auditions.

Only Eden Dawson wasn't the only one with this bright idea.

2 Coffee Corridor

Eden's shoes squeaked on the polished floor as she dashed towards Coffee Corridor, looking for any sign of teachers.

At one end of Coffee Corridor was the staffroom and at the other was the head teacher Mrs Turner's office. Everyone was always on their best behaviour when walking along Coffee Corridor, and, you guessed it, it *always* smelt of coffee. The scent swirled around Eden's nose, making her feel queasier than ever. She always wondered how teachers could drink the stuff; she sneaked a sip of her mum's fancy frothy-mocha-choco-whadyu-call-it once and almost spat it back in the cup! Who knew something so yummy looking could taste so yucky.

Eden walked quickly; she couldn't hear the usual
teacher chatter, nor the whirring sounds of the printer.
Her heart was beating so fast that the loudest thing she
could hear was the thudding in her chest.

She'd just made it down the stairs when she heard
the rhythmic click-clack of heels tapping the floor.
Eden almost froze on the spot – if that was Mrs Turner, she'd
have some serious explaining to do.

The footsteps drew closer as Eden made it to the bottom
of the stairs.

"Ahhhh!" Eden yelped in shock much to a wide-eyed Daniel's surprise.

"Shhh!" Daniel was scowling at Eden, trying – and failing miserably – to camouflage himself against the wall.

"What are you doing here? Why aren't you at the audition?!" Eden's whispers were breathless with the shock of *nearly* being caught by Mrs Turner, and being spotted by Daniel had her legs wobbling like a jelly.

"Why aren't *you*?!" Daniel whispered, looking over Eden's shoulder, expecting Mrs Turner's polished heels to click-clack into view.

Eden bit down on her nails. "Do you think she heard us?"

Daniel raised an eyebrow.

"Us? She definitely heard you! Come on before we both get into trouble!" Daniel headed towards the doors leading to the playground.

"No, in here!" Eden pointed to a door.

"That's the cleaner's cupboard – isn't it lock—" Before he could finish his sentence, Eden opened the door and bustled inside. Daniel stood back, surprised.

"It isn't the cleaner's cupboard … quick, get in!"

3 The props room

The props room was just as Eden remembered: cluttered, colourful and very dusty. She tried to hold her sneeze, cautious that someone might hear.

Daniel was not so quiet. He released three squeaky sneezes which reminded Eden of her cousin's hamster, Cheesepuff. He wiped his dripping nose on his jacket sleeve, much to Eden's horror.

"Gross!" Eden wrinkled her nose and looked away.

"Allergies – " Daniel sniffed.

He looked around the room, swiping cobwebs out of his face. There was stuff *everywhere*. Plastic boxes filled with costumes and props from last year's play, including a wonky looking robot made out of cardboard and tin foil. Behind it, there was a cardboard structure painted to look like an old wooden boat, with so many holes and cracks it looked more like an ancient artefact.

Daniel wandered around taking it all in. "How did *you* know about this room?" he asked, stifling another sneeze.

Eden hesitated. She could tell Daniel the real reason; that when she first started at Orchard Manor, she'd spent every lunchtime of the first term alone, eating her sandwiches by the window, but she felt too embarrassed.

It hadn't been easy trying to fit in to a new school and leaving all of her friends behind. It hadn't been easy moving home and leaving her dad behind either. When Eden's parents separated, Eden felt like everything had separated around her too. Her school, her friends, even the local ice cream van with the awesome double cones and extra sprinkles.

Eden felt nervous starting at Orchard Manor, but not just a little bit nervous, super-duper nervous. She worried about what her new teachers and classmates would be like, whether she'd like them and whether they'd like *her*. On her first day, she had so many butterflies in her tummy that she felt sick and couldn't eat breakfast. At playtime, when she opened her mouth to introduce herself, her throat dried up and her voice came out in a shaky little squeak, and by lunchtime, she'd broken out in a rash!

She was sitting alone on a bench when her smooth brown face began to itch with red lumps and blotches. It was Mrs Pettigrew who called her mum, convinced she was having an allergic reaction, and after a trip to the doctors, Eden learnt that her rash was something called "hives".

"It's harmless," Dr Okpara said. "It can happen when someone is feeling very anxious and worried." She nodded in Eden's direction. Eden had *most certainly* been feeling both of those things.

Unfortunately, Mrs Pettigrew wasn't the only one who saw Eden's hives in action. A few classmates were convinced it was the measles and made sure the entire class knew about it. No one wanted to sit next to her for weeks.

Eden decided not to tell Daniel the real reason she was familiar with the props room – she thought that he wouldn't understand.

"Well, I was helping Mr Pink tidy up after Art one day and he brought some stuff in here – "

Daniel nodded. The props room was a cool hiding place, but he still wanted to know why Eden wasn't at the audition. *Everyone* was at the audition.

He peered over. "Why were you running down Coffee Corridor?"

"Erm, well, why were *you* by the stairs?" she asked, avoiding his gaze.

Daniel nudged a box with his foot. What would he tell Eden?

The truth was, Daniel actually *wanted* a spot in the summer showcase but he was scared he wouldn't get through the auditions. He wasn't very good at singing or dancing, but he liked telling jokes. What if Mr Pink didn't find his jokes funny, or no one laughed? He'd be booed off the stage and be the laughing stock of the school!

He shook the thought out of his mind. He wanted to be good at something; he wanted to showcase a talent his grandpa would be proud of, but Daniel worried that he had no talent at all!

Daniel's grandpa would always tell him, "It's better to let your worries out than keep them in," but he wasn't sure that he wanted to talk about his feelings – what if no one understood? What if his friends thought he was joking or just being silly – what if they *did* laugh at him?!

15

4 Maybe it's a mouse ...

Rustle rustle.

Eden spun round. "What was that?" she gasped.

Their eyes searched the room; it was hard to tell where the noise was coming from, let alone what was making it.

"Maybe it's a mouse," Daniel whispered, peeping into one of the boxes. He was still looking when Eden spotted something strange behind him. The wonky silver robot started looking even wonkier as it slowly began to tilt forward in his direction.

Eden didn't know whether to run or scream, as she watched it fall in slow motion.

It was Daniel who did all the screaming when he turned and saw the giant foil structure heading towards him. He began pushing it back, whacking it with an old script from the floor.

Eden sprang into action, rushing to help. "Shhh, Daniel! You're going to get us caught!" she winced, pressing her fingers to her lips.

"Yeah, Daniel – shhh!"

Eden and Daniel gasped and looked at each other; then slowly turned and looked at the robot, its shiny head tilted to the side.

It couldn't have been the *robot* … could it? Eden peered behind it.

"Wale?" Eden whispered.

Nestled behind the robot was Wale, looking up at Eden, clutching a book.

Wale was known for being the shyest yet smartest kid in the school year. Some kids called him a loner and said he had more books than friends, which was true! He spent most playtimes with his head buried in a book away from the crowds, but that wasn't because he didn't *want* to have friends; Wale just wasn't interested in playing football like the others, not when there was a good book to read. Wale wondered whether he'd ever fit in at Orchard Manor; sometimes he worried that he may never make any friends at all.

"Wale! You were hiding here the whole time?" Daniel squealed in disbelief.

"Yeah, what are you two doing in here?" Wale asked.

But before anyone could answer, they heard shuffling at the door. There was no time to hide; it flew open to reveal a very concerned looking Mrs Pettigrew.

"What on earth are you all doing in here?"

19

Mrs Pettigrew delivered them to Coffee Corridor and fetched Mr Pink, who looked very disappointed.

"You know, I expected more from the three of you," Mr Pink said, tutting. "The summer showcase is such an exciting event for you and your families, I thought you might all want to get involved! But since you would rather be off the stage than on it, Mrs Turner and I have decided you can help build it."

"Build it?" Daniel asked, confused.

"Why yes. We've decided to have a theme for
the summer showcase this year. A backdrop, decorations
– the lot! But *you* will have to decide what that theme is.
We want something extraordinary – truly *out of this world.*"
Mr Pink's eyes sparkled as he spoke, a wide smile parting
his lips.

"We don't have long till showtime, so you'll have plenty
to do – I'm sure you can come up with something grand!"

5 Something extraordinary

Back in the props room, Eden watched Wale in fascination as he folded bits of paper into neat aeroplanes and dainty boats. Wale was relieved when Mr Pink tasked them with set design for the showcase; he much preferred being behind-the-scenes creating things than on the stage.

"If only creating something extraordinary was that simple," Daniel grumbled, prodding at the tattered boat behind them.

Eden suddenly had an idea. "That's it, Daniel! What about *The Isle of Gold*?"

"*The Isle of Gold*?"

"It's the play we went to see at the theatre for our spring term class trip – the one with the talking dreamboat and treasure," said Wale.

Eden nodded enthusiastically. "Yes, that's it! And it was definitely out of this world. Maybe we could recreate it for the showcase?"

Daniel didn't look so sure.

"How do we turn this old thing into a *dream*boat?
It looks more like a shipwreck!"

Daniel kicked the side of the boat, but his foot got firmly
wedged in the cardboard, creating a hole. He tried to pull it
out, but the more he resisted, the more the boat rattled and
shook; it rocked as if it was on the sea!

"I'm stuck!" Daniel panicked, pushing against the boat.

Wale and Eden rushed over to help pull Daniel free,
only the more they pulled, the more stuck Daniel became.

They broke into a sweat, the boat rocking a little harder
and looming a little further over them with each tug until …

CRASH!

6 Shipwrecked!

Daniel opened his eyes and blinked hard, convinced he must be dreaming.

The last thing he remembered was the boat landing on top of them, but now they were covered in fine, golden sand, the sun blazing from the sky above. Surrounding them were tall palm trees swaying in the breeze, and deep blue sea for miles, a far cry from the dusty old props room.

Eden clutched at the warm sand beneath her as she looked around, and there on the shore, just a few steps away, was the boat, looking less like a cardboard prop and more like an old shipwreck!

"What in the world – " she squeaked, her mouth as dry as the sand she was sitting on.

Daniel gasped. "Look!" he said pointing at a tree with a crooked sign attached. "The Isle of Gold!"

"W-what?" Eden stammered in confusion, staring at the sign. "B-b-ut how? When? And where is Wale?"

Eden and Daniel both called for Wale, shouting as loudly as they could.

"It's just a dream; it's just a dream," Daniel whispered under his breath, looking around, trying to make sense of what was happening.

Eden walked closely behind him. *It must be a dream*, she thought to herself, nibbling at her nails, her stomach in knots; but how could she and Daniel both be having the same dream?!

A pile of wide shiny leaves and abandoned planks of wood scattered the island. Daniel spotted a trail of prints in the sand, leading into the trees.

They both looked ahead and gulped. Neither of them wanted to head into the trees with their huge leaves and arching canopies; there was no telling what lurked in there, but Wale was missing. They had to look for him.

"It's no use, you'll never find him in there!" a loud shaky voice cried out from behind them. Eden and Daniel jumped out of their skins, petrified.

Daniel's knees began to buckle. He remembered *The Isle of Gold* play had creatures in it – maybe even an army of killer crabs! What if they were here on the island?! Eden stood frozen beside him, afraid to turn around.

The loud voice cleared its throat. "Ahem – I said it's no use. You'll never find him in there!" It was much steadier now, demanding their attention.

Daniel and Eden slowly turned round, scanning the shore ahead, but there was no one there.

The only thing Eden and Daniel could see ahead was the rickety old boat, beached up on the shore, waves crashing against its side.

"Maybe there's someone in there," Daniel said, in a low hush.

"But who?" Eden squeaked. "That didn't sound like Wale!"

They walked over, toes sinking into the sand as they approached the boat. It creaked loudly, jets of water gushing in through its holes.

The front of the boat stood much taller than Daniel and Eden. They would have to wade into the sea and climb over the side in order to peer in.

Eden began to tip-toe into the water. The boat made another loud groan, the wood creaking against the tide.

"Wait!" shouted Daniel, eyes panicked. He began to walk backwards, lifting his feet high off the sand so quickly that he almost fell on his bottom.

He was pointing at the sand, and at first Eden couldn't see what he was looking at, but emerging from the sea and crawling up the shore were crabs. Lots and lots of crabs.

Eden squealed and clambered into the boat.

"Ow! I know I'm a wreck, but please – be gentle with me!"

Eden almost jumped back into the water! She spun around looking to see where the voice had come from. She gasped – the boat! It was *just* like the play – the "dreamboat" could talk!

Back on the sand, crabs were assembling in rows, their claws clattering as they moved.

Daniel noticed one in particular, waving its large pincers in the air, marching towards him.

"Yes, yes, make way, make way. Captain Clawdia here."

Captain Clawdia, a blue and orange crab with very large pincers, stood inspecting Daniel. "Another intruder?! This small human has come to claim our gold! Prepare to battle fellow comrades."

Daniel shook his head frantically. "Me? No, no, I don't want your gold, I don't even know how we got here!"

"Oh, you don't, hmm?" Captain Clawdia stepped closer. "Then how do you explain old Dreamboat over there?"

31

Daniel glanced over at the old rickety boat, trying to spot Eden.

"I promise, I have no idea – we were in the props room and then … I-I was just hoping to find my friend so we can get back home." Daniel was so nervous that his words were a jumble.

"Your friend?" Captain Clawdia tapped a leg on the sand.

One of the smaller crabs stepped up. "I think he means the prisoner, Captain!"

"*Prisoner?*" Daniel gnawed at his lip; they must be talking about Wale!

"Your friend is an intruder! We heard all of
the commotion. The time portal makes an awful racket
when it's activated – it shakes up the whole island!
We captured him when you both were fast asleep on this
here shore. He was awake and must have figured things
out rather quickly, that clever human. He had spoken to
Dreamboat and had started gathering resources when
we caught him, carrying leaves and wood and digging in
the sand! He was clearly looking for the treasure!"

Daniel stood trying to wrap his head around
everything Captain Clawdia had just said. A portal?
A talking boat? Treasure?

"Please, Captain, he wasn't after your treasure. You have to release him!" Daniel pleaded.

Captain Clawdia let out a surprisingly loud laugh for a crab. "You are funny, aren't you! If you want the prisoner, you'll have to claim him back."

"What? B-but how?" Daniel asked. He wished Eden could hear this, but she was obviously still on the boat.

Captain Clawdia sniffed. "Why, through battle, of course."

Daniel gulped. How would he be able to battle an entire army of crabs?

Captain Clawdia continued. "You see, Intruder … I'm a crab of honour. A captain famed for her intelligence and strategy!" She snapped her large pincers, making Daniel jump. "This is not a mere battle of the claw. *This* is a battle far stronger than that. This is a battle of the *mind!*"

The army cheered in agreement, as Daniel watched them scatter, kicking up sand. They crawled to the shoreline, leaving only Captain Clawdia standing in the middle of what appeared to be a giant grid drawn in the sand.

"I challenge you, Intruder, to a battle of Tic-Tac-Toe and should you defeat me … I'll let your prisoner go."

8 Dreamboat doom

Eden never dreamt in a million years that she would be talking to a boat; in fact, she was still convinced this was all a dream!

Dreamboat told Eden everything that Daniel had now discovered from Captain Clawdia, as she swayed with dizziness, stunned to learn that it was Daniel's kick that had activated the time portal.

Little did Eden know, the Battle of Tic-Tac-Toe was about to begin; it was Dreamboat who warned her.

"It's no use," Dreamboat creaked. "Your friend will never defeat Clawdia – she's too clever. We're doomed, I tell you!"

Eden worried that Dreamboat may be right, but she knew that they had to at least try! Something her dad had once said rang through her head. "Eden, you're braver than you believe, stronger than you seem and smarter than you think!"

She had to help Daniel. They couldn't stay here forever!

9 The Battle of Tic-Tac-Toe

Captain Clawdia and Daniel were deep in battle; Daniel almost didn't notice when Eden came running, making her way to the front of the crowd.

Daniel worried that he wouldn't make the right move. He thought about the times he had played Tic-Tac-Toe with his grandpa, and the special tricks his grandpa had used to win, but he was so nervous that he couldn't even remember them! His nerves made his thoughts such a blur that he struggled to think clearly.

Clawdia drew another circle in the sand with her claw – one more move and she could win!

Daniel looked up and saw what looked like a hundred eyes watching him, including Eden's who gave him a wobbly thumbs up. He began to sweat.

"You can do it, Daniel!" Eden yelled.

But what if he couldn't do it and they were stuck on the island with Wale held prisoner forever?

As if Eden had read his mind, her voice rang out loud and clear: "You're braver than you believe and smarter than you think!"

Daniel took a deep breath. He was so nervous that he felt sick, but he knew he had to try. He stepped forward and drew a cross in the sand.

Captain Clawdia was stumped. She shuffled to the left and shifted to the right before finally drawing another circle in the sand. The crabs gasped.

Clawdia cleared her throat defeatedly. "Well. It appears we have a victor."

Daniel looked confused. "Who's Victor? My name's Daniel."

Eden began squealing, "No, Daniel! She means a victor because you claimed the victory. You did it – you won!"

"Oh! I knew that," Daniel exclaimed, blushing.

Daniel was so relieved he felt like he could float. Even with his blurry thoughts, in the face of what looked like a gazillion crabs, he didn't allow his nerves to get the better of him. He beamed with pride; a broad smile spread across his face.

Captain Clawdia released Wale, who came wandering out of the trees lead by Clawdia's army. Eden and Daniel rushed and hugged him, the three toppling over.

"Wale! Are you all right?! What was it like back there? Are you hurt?" Eden and Daniel talked over each other, bombarding Wale with questions.

Wale smiled shyly and adjusted his glasses. "I'm fine. I'll tell you all about Clawdia's army later, but we have to fix Dreamboat now or we won't get back!"

10 A nervous wreck

The trio were hard at work trying to fix Dreamboat so that they could get back home.

"You're wasting your time. I'm a wreck – a nervous wreck, in fact!"

"But you're a boat, surely sailing is what you're good at?" said Daniel.

"Try sailing with cracks and holes. I don't have what it takes to be a Dreamboat, I'm useless," Dreamboat creaked.

"Well, that isn't true – thanks to Wale's handiwork, no water will be able to get in!" Daniel remarked; he didn't like to hear Dreamboat speak so poorly of itself.

Eden nodded. "Yeah! Besides, you thought Daniel battling Captain Clawdia was useless too, but he won!"

Wale chimed in, "I think we're all good at something, Dreamboat – right guys?"

Daniel paused. The whole reason why he avoided the auditions was because he didn't think he was good at anything. He was so nervous that people would laugh at him, he'd decided to hide. He realised that Wale might be right; maybe we're all good at something after all.

Dreamboat sighed loudly. "Well, what are you all good at then?"

Eden paused. "I can sing."

"You can?" they exclaimed in unison.

Eden nodded, her stomach doing flips. Despite the fact that she loved to sing, it was exactly the reason why she hid from the auditions. The thought of everyone staring at her, like they did on her very first day, made her feel queasy all over again. She was so worried about everyone else's thoughts, that she almost forgot about her own and how much she'd love to sing at the showcase!

Daniel scrunched his eyebrows in confusion. "Well why didn't you go to the auditions?"

Eden wrung her hands. "Because I was scared of singing in front of the whole school."

Daniel looked surprised. He had no idea that Eden felt nervous *or* scared about the auditions. Maybe if they'd spoken about their feelings, they would've realised that they weren't alone.

"You know, Eden, someone once told me that you're braver than you believe," Daniel said, giving her a nudge.

Eden smiled; maybe she *was* braver than she thought she was!

11 All aboard!

"Wale, how did you know how to patch me up?" croaked Dreamboat.

Wale pushed his glasses up his nose. "Oh, I read it somewhere. I like to build and fix things – I hope to be an engineer someday."

"That's so cool, Wale," gushed Eden. "You'd be a great one too!"

Wale smiled sheepishly, a warm glow rising to his cheeks. No one had ever said that to him before; certainly no one from Orchard Manor. It felt nice to be complimented.

They looked at Daniel who felt his mouth go dry. "Your turn," said Dreamboat.

Daniel paused. "Well, I don't know if I'm good at anything. That's why I didn't go to the audition. I wanted to but I was scared everyone would laugh at me."

"*You* were *scared*?" Eden said, shocked. "But you've been so brave! *You* were the one who defeated Captain Clawdia and her army!"

"Yeah, Daniel, if it wasn't for you, then I'd still be held prisoner," said Wale.

Daniel blushed. "Grandpa always told me that friends don't leave friends behind. I had to try, so that we could all get home," he said, smiling at Wale and Eden who beamed back.

Wale was smiling so hard that his cheeks ached, but he didn't mind. All this time he'd worried he would never make any friends, and yet, today, he'd made two. It truly felt like a dream!

Eden, Daniel and Wale had all been so nervous hiding in the props room, when really, they had all been a lot braver than they realised. After the day they'd had, the auditions didn't seem so bad after all.

Eden had a thought. "When we get back, I'm going to ask Mr Pink if I can join the showcase!" she exclaimed.

Daniel's eyes lit up. "Me too!" He paused. "You know, Dreamboat, if we can fight our worries and win, then you can too!"

Wale nodded. "It's true, Dreamboat! It's OK to feel down, or nervous; just remember that feelings can change! You may feel down now but it doesn't mean you'll feel that way forever. I never guessed I'd make friends on the Isle of Gold, but here they are!" His eyes gleamed as he spoke.

The three had shown Dreamboat courage, but also what it truly meant to believe in each other and themselves, even when feeling afraid. It was just the boost that Dreamboat needed.

Dreamboat cleared its throat. "Well then, in that case – all aboard, Worry Warriors! Destination: Orchard Manor! We have a showcase to attend!"

12 Teamwork dreamwork

The three got to work and it wasn't long before they had created a set design for the showcase that truly was extraordinary. Wale painted Dreamboat in a gorgeous, glittering gold and had even recreated Captain Clawdia's army, folding card into little crabs, which Eden helped to paint.

"Oh my!" Mr Pink beamed, rubbing his hands excitedly as he entered the props room. "Well, isn't this just excellent! The three of you have exceeded yourselves; teamwork really does make the dreamwork!" He laughed heartily.

"Now, Wale said something about his two talented friends wanting to perform in the showcase?"

Eden and Daniel grinned, looking over at Wale who nodded encouragingly.

Eden spoke first. "Is it too late to get a slot for the showcase, Mr Pink?"

Mr Pink paused for a moment. "Well, given that you've all done such an excellent job, I think I can manage to squeeze you both in," he winked.

51

13 Showtime

It was the night of the showcase and the school hall was buzzing with excitement.

Eden's tummy fluttered with butterflies, but rather than feeling sick, she felt excited. She took deep breaths and peeped from behind the curtain to see the audience. Dreamboat stood bold on the stage, glowing under the spotlights.

A nervous Daniel stood beside Eden, gnawing his bottom lip. He gulped. "Woah, that's a *lot* of people."

Eden nodded and squeezed his sweaty palm. "Just pretend they're crabs."

They looked at each other and burst into a fit of giggles.

Daniel remembered just how proud he'd felt to win the battle of Tic-Tac-Toe, despite his nerves. If he could do that, then he could certainly perform at the showcase.

"Ready, Worry Warriors?" asked Wale, cheerily behind them. "Just wanted to wish you good luck – not that you'll need it! It's OK to feel nervous, just remember, you're braver than you believe. You've got this!"

They nodded and smiled at each other; they'd come a long way from hiding in the props room!

The audience lights dimmed and Mr Pink took to the stage. He tapped the microphone. "Welcome all, to the most extraordinary event of the year. Let the show begin!"

The Worry Warriors' journey